Dare to be Naughty

Masters Club Series – Book 3.5

CLAIRE THOMPSON

Edited by Jae Ashley

Chapter 1

Dahlia Simon hurtled into the staff cafeteria, not even stopping by her office first to drop off her coat. Plastic pine boughs threaded with tinsel and shiny red and green ornaments had been hung along one wall in a nod to the season, a small menorah set on a table beneath. As she caught her breath, she scanned the room, trying to distinguish among the various white-coated and scrubs-clad people hunched over their breakfast trays.

Where was Hayden? Had she missed him? Had he even been there? Had she ruined everything?

Her heart lifted, relief flooding her when she spied him at a table in the corner, his back to her. She stood still a moment, drinking him in. Even from behind, he was easy on the eyes, his wavy light brown hair streaked with gold and in perpetual need of a cut. She liked it that way, curling against the back of his neck in pleasing contrast to the dark blue scrubs that stretched across his broad shoulders and back. Not that she'd ever tell him that. Guys as good looking as Hayden Pierce needed no additional encouragement.

Moving toward the self-serve area, she grabbed a yogurt and a bottle of water, paid for her purchases and headed toward his table. As she approached, she saw he was on his cell, his tone quiet but earnest. She naturally assumed he was talking to a patient or another doctor. As she got closer, she froze in place, immobilized by what she was hearing.

"...might want to consider restraining her for the needle play. Ropes—chains—whatever makes sense. If you take away that added difficulty of requiring her to hold her own position, she might be better able to fully embrace her submission."

Goose bumps prickled over Dahlia's skin. What in the world was the man talking about? And to whom?

Hayden turned, catching sight of her as she neared. "Gotta go," he said abruptly. "Keep me posted."

Without missing a beat, he flashed a smile at Dahlia while slipping his cell into his pocket. "There you are," he said easily, his expression friendly but neutral. "Thought I was going to have to finish my breakfast alone this morning."

Setting down her tray, she removed her coat,

draping it over the back of the chair. Her carefully rehearsed apology had flown from her brain, his words of a moment before crowding it out.

Ropes. Chains. Submission…

Hayden was regarding her curiously, apparently waiting for some kind of response.

"Sorry I was so late," she managed as she slid into the seat across from his at the small table. "I got to my subway stop just as my train was pulling away and had to wait over twenty minutes for the next one."

He nodded sympathetically as he speared a large bite of pancake soaked in butter and syrup. He didn't seem to be in the least bit perturbed. Was she the only one who'd spent the weekend ruminating over the train wreck of what had been a promising conversation that past Friday? Maybe she'd made a bigger thing of it all than it had warranted.

As she opened her yogurt, her thoughts were again hijacked by the overheard snippet of conversation just now.

Having learned the hard way to maintain boundaries at work, Dahlia routinely discouraged male colleagues with other ideas. But Hayden was different. He didn't come on to her with sleazy innuendo or awkward attempts at flirtation. Nor did he make any of those subtle digs or snarky insinuations so many guys, threatened by a successful, accomplished woman, felt compelled to make. He was confident without being arrogant, supportive without being condescending.

In the three months since she'd moved to New York and joined the Mount Sinai staff as an orthopedic surgeon, Hayden and she had evolved from work colleagues into friends. From the first, a flame of mutual attraction had smoldered just beneath the surface, though it had yet to segue into something more.

In the brief time they'd known one another, Hayden had made it clear he respected her as a doctor and an equal. In fact, that was how they'd first connected—he'd sought out her professional opinion on a particularly complicated surgical case. They'd met in the doctor's cafeteria to discuss the case.

They'd ended up lingering over breakfast, their conversation edging into the personal. Before heading off to their respective floors, they'd agreed to meet again each Monday morning before rounds.

As the weeks passed, though they continued only to meet for breakfast, casual flirting began to cross the line into something with the potential for more. A shared look would be held several beats too long, something passing between them that made her pulse quicken. Or their fingertips might brush as one passed salt to the other, and his touch would fizz along her skin like champagne bubbles.

Dahlia wasn't a woman given to crushes or casual dating. Her last boyfriend had been during her second year of medical school. Her entire adult life had been focused on getting her medical degree and then scrabbling for position in the very competitive, still-male-dominated field of orthopedic surgery.

Yet, with Hayden, she was able to let down her guard. There was something about him—something commanding but nurturing—that spoke to her softer, hidden nature, one she revealed to no one. At the same time, the understated dominance he exhibited could be unsettling. She would catch him regarding her with an edgy, sexy gaze that seemed to strip her bare. Perhaps it was that combination of good guy/bad boy that so attracted her.

Then she'd gone and fucked everything up.

It had happened the previous Friday. They'd agreed to meet at an impromptu happy hour put together by some of their colleagues. At first, things had gone better than she could have hoped for. Hayden was already there when she arrived, and had saved a place for her at the table. Over mugs of beer and greasy bar snacks, their ongoing flirtation took a decidedly more intense turn. Their banter had been drenched in playful sexual innuendo, their attention solely on each other.

They'd been talking about relationships, and how awkward that "first time" could be. When he'd reached out and touched her neck lightly with his fingertip, drawing it sensually down to her clavicle, she'd momentarily forgotten how to breathe.

While she was still reeling from the power of his touch, he'd fixed her with a smoldering gaze. In a casual tone that belied the dark glint in his eyes, he'd said with a slow, sexy smile, "I like to break the ice with some bondage and a good hard spanking."

Something deep inside her had ignited in a whoosh at his startling words. Heat had rushed to her face, her nipples tightening, her pulse suddenly racing.

She'd read plenty of novels dealing with alpha males who dominated submissive women, bending both their minds and bodies to their masterful wills. She'd even allowed herself to imagine what it would be like to be "owned" by another person, sexually speaking—to give herself completely to another, surrendering full control.

But she'd always relegated these sexual fantasies firmly to masturbatory fodder. They didn't jibe with her notion of herself as a strong, independent woman. There was no way she'd subjugate herself to some man, no matter how secretly enticing the idea of submission might be.

Yet, Hayden's comment had tilted her world suddenly on its axis, tapping directly into fantasies she barely permitted herself to consider, except when alone at night in her bed, hand between her legs. Momentarily disarmed, she'd fallen back on sarcasm to hide her discomfiture.

"Talk about a sexist caveman fantasy," she'd retorted scathingly. "Give me a break."

Hayden had looked for a moment as if he'd been slapped, but he'd quickly recovered. He'd tilted his head, looking past her face and directly into her soul. "Who's to judge another person's innermost yearnings, hmm?" he'd queried in that deep, silky voice of his.

She'd been embarrassed at his gentle rebuke and chagrined by the blush she'd felt splashing over her cheeks. Again she opened her mouth, inserting her foot once more with yet another stupid remark, this one about frightened little boys resorting to physical force to keep their own insecurities at bay.

Something in his face closed then, as if a gate had suddenly been lowered between them. The easy, sexy mood of a moment before was destroyed, and she was to blame.

The really crazy part was that she had known, even as the words tumbled like toads from her mouth, that she wasn't being honest.

Something inside her—that secret inner voice that whispered below the radar of her self-imposed censorship—had come alive at his words. *Yes*, it had breathed. *I've been waiting for you. Tell me more...*

At the time, she'd been too confused by her own conflicting feelings to do or say anything that might have salvaged the situation. The damage had been done. Hayden had made his excuses soon thereafter, leaving her frustrated and furious with herself.

Now, as she regarded the handsome man across the breakfast table, she wondered how she could bring back that spark without making herself too vulnerable in the process. Snippets from his phone conversation of a few moments before replayed in her mind, adding a dark, mysterious element to the mix. Was there a connection between his remark at the happy hour and whatever the hell it was she'd overheard?

Restrain her...needle play...ropes, chains, submission...

As at the happy hour, his provocative words, though clearly not meant for her ears, had instantly penetrated her defenses, making her heart race and her nipples tingle. This was her chance to make it right. Or at least to open the door again...

Before she could talk herself out of it, Dahlia blurted, "I heard you, you know. Just now, I mean. I heard what you were saying. Based on your comment the other night, I'm guessing that wasn't some kind of medieval medical treatment you were discussing."

She held her breath in anticipation of his response. Was she ready for his answer, whatever it might be?

Would he be angry that she'd eavesdropped on his private conversation?

When he didn't respond right away, she lifted her water bottle to her lips to hide her embarrassment, flustered to see her hand was shaking. She put down the bottle, gripping her hands in her lap as she struggled for control.

When she raised her eyes to his face, she was startled to see he didn't look upset or the slightest bit self-conscious, or concerned he'd been overheard. Instead, he lifted one brow, an ironic smile ghosting his lips. "Curious about the sexist caveman's private conversation?"

She winced at the reminder.

"Be careful, little girl," he added teasingly, though she sensed the steel beneath his words. "You really shouldn't ask questions you don't actually want answered."

"Little girl?" she countered. She'd meant for a sassy retort, but the quaver in her voice gave her away. Swallowing hard, she pushed on, "I wouldn't have asked if I didn't want to know."

His eyes slid down to her chest, lingering there for an insolent moment before returning lazily to her face. Her nipples, taut now to the point of throbbing, had to be visible beneath her scrubs. She clenched her hands, refusing to give him the satisfaction of covering herself as she tried to maintain a calm, confident gaze.

He regarded her for a long moment. Something in his gaze sent a shiver of raw desire directly to her sex.

She drew in a deep breath, determined to plow on. Now that she'd taken this step, no way was she going to retreat. She managed an answering grin. "It's okay, Hayden. I get it if you're embarrassed and uncomfortable about your, uh, kink."

"Not at all. I'm just a little surprised, frankly, that you're interested, after Friday night."

His words hit home, despite his teasing tone. Why was she being so flippant? She needed to drop the sarcasm if she wanted an honest answer.

She looked down at the table. "About that. I want to apologize. I think I was just so taken by surprise that I resorted to snark. Your comment startled me."

It had done a whole lot more than that. She bit her lower lip, determined to be more honest. Lifting her head, she met his eye. "Then, overhearing that snippet of conversation about...whatever it was about... I was intrigued by what you said because it touched something in me. I...I sometimes have fantasies..."

Oh god. Why was this so hard? Just say it already.

"The thought of a strong guy—an alpha guy taking

what he wants sexually—that turns me on." Suddenly afraid she'd revealed too much, she added quickly, "Academically speaking, of course."

Hayden's eyebrows rose high on his forehead, his lips quirking in a sardonic smile. "You give with one hand and take with the other," he teased. "Okay, then, Dr. Simon. In the interest of academics, if you're sure you want to know what I was discussing in my private conversation…"

Fighting down the blush that tried to invade her face, Dahlia replied, "Yes. I do. Please."

"Okay then. Full disclosure. I'm into something called BDSM. The acronym stands for bondage, discipline or dominance, sadism or submission and masochism."

"I know what it stands for," Dahlia replied a little too quickly. She bit her lip to keep from interrupting again.

"Good to hear," Hayden said with apparent approval.

The blush won, heat rushing full-force into her cheeks.

"I'm what you'd call a sensual sadist," Hayden continued. "I get off on inflicting erotic pain and exerting complete sexual control over another human being, though only with their full consent and desire. What you heard on the phone—that was a fellow Dom in need of some advice about training a new submissive. We both belong to a private club that caters to this particular lifestyle."

"For real?" Dahlia squeaked, her normally low-pitched voice suddenly an octave higher. A private BDSM club? Clearly, Hayden was into way more than a bit of bondage and a playful spanking!

Not yet ready to confront him directly about his predilections, she offered instead, "I've heard of those underground BDSM clubs, but I figured they were just skeevy pickup joints with a theme. There are actual private clubs for that kind of thing?"

"There are private clubs, and then there's this particular club, which as far as I know, is quite unique. Members are only admitted after rigorous assessment of their dedication and understanding of the lifestyle, and that includes Doms as well as subs. This is a lot more than just an exclusive, private dungeon for folks to massage their kink. It's about a lot more than just whips and chains, I assure you. We explore the passion and power of erotic submission on a number of levels—everything from casual play to full-on slave training. Your remark the other night about cavemen notwithstanding, true D/s isn't about subjugation. Not at all. It's a free and loving exchange of power—the most intense, absorbing exchange possible between two human beings, at least for those hardwired for the experience."

Dahlia was quiet as she pondered his words. She could feel his unspoken power pulling her toward him as if he were the flame and she the moth. While her brain cautioned her from stepping into dangerous waters, the rest of her had other ideas.

"I want to go," she blurted, surprising herself not only with her forwardness, but with how very much she meant it. "Can I come with you? I want to go to your club and see for myself."

Hayden shook his head, though he was smiling. "Sorry. No can do. I've already said too much as it is. As for you coming to take a peek, that would never fly. Only members or prospective members are granted admittance."

Suddenly he furrowed his brow, pursing his lips in apparent thought. "Except..." He trailed off, then shook his head. "Nah. Not a good idea."

"What?" she insisted. "What isn't a good idea? What were you going to say? Finish the sentence. Except...?"

Hayden met her gaze with a small shrug. "Okay, okay. I was going to say, except for the one time during the year when we make an exception. In fact, it's right around the corner. Guests are permitted at our annual holiday party, which happens to be a week from this Saturday. That said, I don't really think it's something you would want to attend. It's not for—"

"I do want to attend," she interrupted, aware she was being pushy, but unable to help herself. "Come on, Hayden. You can't throw something like that out there and then pull it back. I'm wildly curious now."

He studied her while he weighed his response. She held her breath, willing him to say yes.

Finally, he said, "Academic curiosity is all very well, Dahlia, but this event is something else again. We are not talking about a Christmas party with a kinky theme. Not by a long shot."

"So, enlighten me," she urged, more intrigued than ever. "Let me make an informed decision before I say yes or no."

Hayden chuckled, shaking his head. "So sorry. The decision isn't yours to make." He smiled to soften his words. "I haven't yet extended the invitation. It was indiscreet of me even to bring up the possibility."

"Come on, Hayden. Please," she cajoled in a wheedling tone, her curiosity raging. "Don't be such a tease. At least tell me what it is I'd be missing."

"Fair enough," he finally replied. "I've let the cat out of the bag, so no harm in sharing a little more detail, I suppose. I trust all of this will remain strictly between us."

"Of course," Dahlia readily agreed, trying to tamp

down her excitement. She drew her finger across her lips. "My lips are sealed." Crossing her arms over her chest, she added with a grin, "Cross my heart and hope to die."

Hayden chuckled. "All right, all right. Don't say I didn't warn you." He lowered his voice so she had to lean across the table to hear him. "Our members engage in serious, hardcore, explicit BDSM play. If you were to attend the party, while you wouldn't be required to actively participate, you'd be witness to bondage, impact play, extreme submission, nudity and overt sexual acts. What we do is one-hundred-percent consensual, but it's not a game. Not for us. It's serious business—the essence of who we are."

"Gosh," Dahlia blurted, both shocked and thrilled.

Did she really want to get within a mile of such a place? While her brain attempted to dismiss the whole thing out of hand, her body had other ideas. There was a definite damp spot spreading in the crotch of her panties, and her nipples were so hard they almost hurt. And that secret, barely acknowledged part of her soul was melting with longing for something she'd never quite dared to articulate.

And this was Hayden she was talking to, not some creepy guy at a bar, or some unreliable source on the internet. Everything she knew about Hayden Pierce spoke to his integrity and goodness. If he was involved with this club, there had to be more to it.

"Gosh," she repeated. "I never imagined such a place could exist, except in novels."

"Novels you've read?" Hayden queried, fixing her with a curious gaze.

"Well, um, yes," she admitted, her eyes flitting away from his. "Romance novels. They're my escape. Well," she amended, determined to be honest, "romance novels with a BDSM twist. And sometimes fantasy abduction stories."

Hayden's eyes hooded in a sexy way as he regarded her. Then, slowly, deliberately, he reached his hand across the small table and ran his finger lightly down her bare arm, his eyes on hers all the while.

His touch left a trail of heat in its wake, and her body responded with a shudder of desire she couldn't suppress. She had a sudden insane desire to grab his hand and kiss his palm, right there in the staff cafeteria.

Instead, she pushed on. "So, you see? I'm not some totally clueless vanilla girl. I already know all about this stuff and I'm totally cool with it. I'd love a chance to see what it's like in real life."

Hayden's smile was amused. "Sorry to burst your bubble, but reading fiction does not mean you know much of anything." He chuckled. "Still, you're nothing if not persistent, I'll give you that."

He paused while she held her breath. Finally, he said, "If we were to extend an invitation, you'd be required to sign a comprehensive non-disclosure agreement both about the club's existence and anything you see there. As you might imagine, we guard our privacy very carefully, for obvious reasons."

"Done," she said promptly.

"Assuming we get that far," Hayden countered, "on this one night everyone attending the party is required to wear a masquerade mask at all times. You may remove the rest of your clothing, but the mask is to remain in place, no exceptions."

You may remove the rest of your clothing…

Dahlia realized her mouth was hanging open, and she snapped it shut. Was this more than she could handle, academically or otherwise? Should she admit defeat and say thanks but no thanks?

Yet, even as she considered this option, her entire body thrummed with excitement. Her nipples continued to tent her top, while her panties were now soaked, her clit throbbing. As crazy as it was to admit, rather than scaring her away, he'd only stoked the fires of her curiosity and secret longing.

Hayden's cell phone chirped in his pants pocket, startling Dahlia from her brief reverie. He pulled it out and examined the screen. "Uh oh," he said, pushing back from the table. "I'm late for rounds. Gotta go."

"Wait," Dahlia cried, her mind suddenly made up. "You can't just walk away without resolving this. Come on, Hayden. I'm cool with everything you've said, I swear it. I'll sign whatever you want, and adhere to all the rules, I promise. I really, really want to go to that party. Please."

She held her breath, willing him to agree.

He turned back, fixing her once more with his penetrating gaze. "I believe you actually mean it. Or think you do."

"I do," Dahlia asserted emphatically, ignoring the butterflies flitting wildly in her stomach.

"I'll consider it," he said lightly. "Have a great day, Dr. Simon."

Chapter 2

Hayden bounced lightly on the balls of his feet as he waited in the lobby of Dahlia's apartment building. He felt slightly off-balance, emotionally speaking. It was a new feeling for him. Both as a doctor and as a Head Master at the Masters Club, he was used to being in full control, not only of the situation, but of himself.

Had he let his growing attraction for the lovely Dahlia obscure his better judgment? After all, she had sent mixed messages about her actual interest in BDSM. Was she just curious, or was there genuine submissive desire lurking beneath her sassy exterior?

Tonight, he intended to find out.

It was Friday evening, the first moment since Monday morning they'd managed to find the time between their busy schedules to meet again. They had made arrangements to go for dinner at a bistro she liked near her apartment. He was looking very much forward to seeing her again, away from the hospital.

As he'd promised, Hayden had given some thought—plenty of it, actually—to the idea of inviting Dahlia to the Masters Club holiday party. Typically, when non-members were invited, they were already quite active in the BDSM scene, their own sexual orientation as Dom or sub clearly established.

He'd basically had no business dangling the possibility of an invitation to a complete novice. It had just...happened.

It wasn't only her good looks that attracted him, though they were considerable. Of medium height, she had small, high breasts and a long, slender waist that flared into curvaceous hips. Always in scrubs, often covered by a lab coat, he had yet to properly assess her ass, but he could see by the way it filled out her scrub bottoms that it was ample and well-shaped—perfect for spanking.

At work, she wore her hair scraped back in a no-nonsense ponytail, no discernible makeup on her face. Not that she needed any, with that creamy complexion and those large hazel eyes fringed with thick, dark blond lashes.

At the happy hour the week before, she'd let her hair down in a shiny tumble of honey-blond waves, and had added a touch of red lipstick to her full, sensual mouth. The effect had been breathtaking, and he definitely wasn't the only guy to notice. But, to his delight, she'd appeared only to have eyes for him.

Their interaction had crackled with possibility, the casual work flirtation edging into new territory that had intrigued him. He'd been turned on by the sexy way she'd ducked her head, color rising in her cheeks when he'd gently teased her. He'd taken note of the submissive way her pupils had dilated. Her sharp intake of breath when he'd run his finger along her silky-soft skin had awoken the Dom in him.

He'd purposely made the comment about bondage and spanking to check her reaction. Her scathing retort had brought things to a screeching halt, at least for him. As much as he was attracted to her, Hayden had long ago learned it was pointless to get involved with a vanilla woman. It never ended well, in spite of everyone's best intentions. He'd resigned himself to return to their more superficial work friend relationship and leave it at that.

Happily, her overhearing him on his cell had been a gift from the BDSM gods. She'd both surprised and delighted him with her avid interest in what she'd heard of his side of the conversation, none of the snarkiness of her previous reaction in her tone. She hadn't realized it, but that chance occurrence had given their potential relationship a crucial jumpstart.

The elevator door opened, pulling Hayden's attention back to the moment. Dahlia emerged, looking radiant. Her eyes, which had always tended toward blue when in her ubiquitous blue scrubs, were now a lovely olive green, her fringe of thick blond lashes darkened with a touch of mascara. She wore a loose-knit, long-sleeved, pale pink sweater over a pair of black slacks that hugged shapely legs, black ankle boots on her feet. A black quilted jacket was slung over one arm. Her hair fell prettily to her shoulders, her lips a glossy pink, her eyes bright.

Resisting the impulse to pull her into his arms and thrust his tongue into her mouth, he instead kissed her chastely on the cheek. "You look beautiful," he said, smiling down at her.

She smiled back, perhaps a little shyly, though her eyes were sparkling. "You don't look so bad yourself."

He grinned. "Thanks." The place they were going was casual, and he'd worn his usual non-work, non-scene outfit of faded jeans, a black, three-quarter-sleeve knit shirt and, because it was chilly outside, his favorite black leather jacket.

"I'm starving," she announced. "How about you? Hungry?"

"Ravenous," he replied, hooding his eyes as he let them trail from her face to her body. Moving closer, he drew his fingertip lightly over her throat as they locked eyes. She responded as he'd hoped, her eyes widening, a slight tremor moving through her frame.

Yes, there was definite potential here, and it was for far more than the "academic" interest she'd professed. Something deeper was driving her, something he very much wanted to explore. Tonight would be the test, assuming things went as planned.

He let his hand fall away and took a step back, breaking the sensual mood that had enveloped them. "Ready?"

Dahlia shook her head, as if emerging from a trance. "Let's do it."

They didn't say much as they navigated their way along the brightly lit, still-crowded New York sidewalks. The air was invigoratingly brisk, the moon visible in the dark sky above the buildings.

She seemed slightly startled when he moved to open the bistro's door for her, as if not used to the polite gesture. "Oh," she said, smiling as she stepped through. "A gentleman. Thank you, sir."

His cock nudged in response to her use of the word "sir," though he understood she was using it in the generic sense, rather than the *Sir* a submissive used when addressing her Dom. His cock stiffened at the sudden vision of her naked and on her knees before him, sweetly replying, "Yes, Sir," to his command.

The hostess led them to a small booth near the back of the restaurant. Once their orders were placed, mugs of beer in front of them, Hayden leaned forward. "You've had a little time to think things over. Do you still want to come to our holiday party?"

"Absolutely," she replied staunchly. "In fact, I've been doing some research in preparation. Real research, I mean. Not just reading more BDSM romance novels."

Hayden smiled, pleased. "Do tell," he encouraged.

"I went online and checked out easily a dozen websites all about BDSM. It was fascinating, reading about real people who actually live the lifestyle, 24/7. I learned the difference between a D/s relationship and a total exchange of power between a Master and a slave. I read a lot about the concept of erotic pain, and its power to transmute into something almost spiritual when the connection is right."

A rosy blush was moving over her cheeks as she spoke, which Hayden found quite adorable. He was tempted to tease her about it, but decided to cut her some slack. The fact she'd spent time learning more about the lifestyle, and that what she'd learned hadn't turned her off, was an excellent sign.

Their food arrived, and they didn't revisit the topic until the waiter brought the check. Dahlia immediately reached for her wallet, but Hayden stopped her. "It's on me tonight. Okay?"

He could see from her expression that she was

gearing up to protest. Like many professional women, especially ones newly successful in their fields, she probably made it a point always to pay her way. Hayden had no problem with that—in a professional situation. But he wanted tonight to feel different—to be different—than any previous interaction between them.

He fixed her with a calm but steady gaze, bending her to his will.

"Okay," she finally said in a soft voice, letting her hand drop. "Thank you."

As he hoped, when they returned to her building lobby, Dahlia said, "Would you like to come upstairs for a bit? Maybe have something to drink before you head home?"

"Sure," he said with a smile. "I'd like that very much."

As they entered her apartment, Dahlia gestured for Hayden to hang his jacket on the coatrack beside the door, and she did the same. The place was small, the furnishings bland but new and clean, nondescript framed artwork on the walls. The only exception was an ancient recliner covered in rich, buttery leather, a butt-shaped dent in the seat from what must be years of sitting. A tottering pile of medical journals lay on the floor beside it, a laptop on top of them.

Noticing him glancing around, she said with a laugh, "It's a furnished rental, decorated in the style of the Holiday Inn Express, or maybe an upscale Motel 8. It was the only thing I could find that was remotely affordable on the subway route to the hospital when I took the job back in October."

"Except that," he grinned, pointing a finger toward her recliner.

"Except that," she agreed. "I got that recliner my first year of medical school at a thrift store, and I've lugged it wherever I go ever since."

"Everyone needs at least one comfy place to crash," Hayden agreed, liking her immensely.

"Wine," she said briskly, as if recalling herself. "White or red? Chardonnay or cabernet? Those are the choices."

"I think I'll just have a glass of ice water," Hayden said. He wanted to be alert for what he had planned. "But, please," he added quickly, "you have a glass if you'd like."

"One glass of ice water coming up," she said with a smile. "Have a seat. I'll bring it out. There's not actually room in my kitchenette for more than one person." She seemed more relaxed now, in her own space. That was good. He wanted her relaxed.

He sat on the couch, leaning back as he waited for Dahlia to return. He was excited about what he had planned. The first step was to get her to agree. It had been a long time since he'd worked with a total newbie.

With those new to the scene, it was sometimes a challenge to tease out genuine submissive emotions buried beneath a lifetime of denial. Yet, he sensed something in Dahlia, something that went beyond the merely curious. Though he knew he would be wise to keep his expectations in check, he couldn't deny his excitement at the opportunity to bring her true nature to the fore.

Dahlia came back into the living room, water in one hand, a glass of white wine in the other. After handing him his glass, she sat beside him. She smelled good—something floral with a bit of spice.

He raised his glass to hers. "To new adventures," he said as they clinked.

"To new adventures," she echoed. "I like that."

"Good," he replied, admiring the long, smooth line of her throat as she sipped her wine. "It'll be quite an adventure, I assure you."

She looked at him expectantly, her eyes bright. "Does that mean you're going to invite me to the party? I get to come?"

He suppressed a grin at the double entendre of her last sentence. "Actually," he said slowly, "that's going to depend on you."

"On me?"

He nodded. "I've done a lot of thinking about this. It was irresponsible of me to dangle that invitation in front of you the way I did, especially knowing you have little to no experience in the scene."

"But I did the research. I've read the novels. I want to go to the party in the worst way—"

He placed two fingers briefly lightly over her lips, silencing her.

"I think your enthusiasm is great. But hear me out before you decide. I have a proposal for you."

She nodded. "Okay. Sorry. I'm listening."

"As I intimated the other day at breakfast, if you attend this party, you'll see things that will shock you. You'll be witness to extreme bondage, whippings, canings, water play and explicit sexual acts. Many of the subs and service slaves will be naked or nearly so, men and women alike."

Dahlia stared at him with wide eyes, her pretty mouth falling partly open. "You, uh—you mentioned at breakfast I wouldn't have to actively participate, right?"

"That's correct. Only if you want to. It's not a decision you need to make now."

She looked relieved. "Okay. Good. So, what's this proposal?"

"I want to invite you to the party. But it wouldn't be fair either to you or to the members of my club to bring in someone who only wants to gawk. That's the opposite of what we've created—which is a sanctuary for hardcore lifestylers. So, in order for me to be comfortable even extending the invitation, I need to get a better sense of your true, personal interest in the scene. In order to do that in the very limited timeframe we have before next weekend, I'd like—with your full consent, of course—to put you through a series of tests designed to better tease out your innate submissive potential."

"Tests?" she repeated, looking mildly alarmed.

"Yes. And I'm afraid this is nonnegotiable. If you're unable or unwilling to do this exercise with me, it's better we just put this behind us and move on."

"Okay," she said slowly. "I'm listening. What do these tests involve exactly? I need details so I can make an informed decision."

"Of course," Hayden agreed, pleased she wasn't put off by the challenge. "To start, I'll ask you a few questions to get a better understanding as to your thoughts and feelings about erotic submission. There are no right or wrong answers, but I will require rigorous honesty on your part. No censoring the replies to protect yourself or to say what you think I might want to hear. I want your genuine, heartfelt response. You good with that?"

"Yes," she agreed readily. "I can totally do that."

"Okay, good. Now it gets a little more complicated. You need to understand up front that this preliminary session will involve you removing some or all of your clothing. I've found potential subs do a lot better when there's literally nothing between them and the Dom. It puts you immediately in a more submissive headspace because of your inherently vulnerable position in front of someone who is fully clothed. With me so far?"

Dahlia was staring at him like a deer caught in the headlights. Yet, her nipples were prominent now beneath the loose knit of her sweater and he could feel her excitement simmering just below the surface. If he placed his hand between her legs, would he find her wet?

When she didn't respond right away, he said gently, "I get it, Dahlia. I'm asking an awful lot of someone who has only second and thirdhand knowledge in the scene. Normally with a potential sub, I'd go a lot slower, giving you a chance to absorb what was happening over time. Unfortunately, given our deadline for the holiday party, we have limited time. If this is too much for you, we can take it slower. We can forget about the party, and just take our time."

"No," she cried. Looking somewhat abashed, she continued, "I mean, yes. Yes, I'm with you. I don't want to slow down. I want to do whatever it takes to attend the party."

"Great," he said, grinning to hide his relief. She was nervous but determined, and he admired that.

Sobering, he added, "The goal tonight is to give me a sense not only of your willingness to obey and submit, but to observe how that submission affects you. Don't worry, this won't involve whips, rope or even a playful spanking. The caveman will remain in his cave."

"Ha," she snorted. "I deserved that."

He waved a dismissive hand. "I'm just teasing you. But seriously, if at any time you're uncomfortable with what's happening and want me to stop, I'll end the session immediately. Like I said, we can always pick things up at a later date, if you're still interested."

"No, I want to see this through," she asserted staunchly. Then she shrugged. "You know what they say—in for a penny, in for a pound. Let's do this thing."

"Let's do it," he agreed. It startled him to realize Dahlia wasn't the only one who was a little nervous. He, too, was out of his comfort zone. As a Head Master, he wasn't used to being the one with anything at stake. Subs came to him for training. He never sought them out.

Something about this enigmatic woman drew him in a way he couldn't remember ever feeling. Whatever happened tonight, it would affect him as much as it affected her. He would need to tread carefully, for both their sakes.

Dahlia was watching him, a tendril of blond hair falling over one eye, the tip of her pink tongue just visible between parted lips. His cock stiffened, his lips tingling with the need to kiss her.

Ignoring his body, he took Dahlia's free hand and looked her in the eye. Her hand trembled ever so slightly in his. He held it gently until the trembling stilled. When she met his eyes, he said, "From this moment until I release you, you will obey my commands to the letter, without question and without hesitation. Do you accept these terms?"

She said nothing for a long moment. Hayden remained absolutely still, his breath held, his heart pausing in its beat. This would only work if she was fully on board.

Finally, Dahlia pulled her hand from his. She placed her wineglass on the end table beside the couch and got to her feet. She lowered herself to her knees on the carpet in front of him, placing her hands on her thighs.

He gasped involuntarily at the lovely and quite

unexpected submissive gesture. She looked sexy as hell as she gazed up at him through her thick lashes. She swallowed visibly, as if gathering her courage.

"Yes," she said at last, her voice quavering ever so slightly. "Yes, Sir. I agree."

Chapter 3

The atmosphere seemed to shift in the room, as if even the air were holding its breath. The nearly constant ping and clang of the ancient cast iron hot water radiator was suddenly silent. Only the sound of her own hammering heart echoed in Dahlia's ears, so loud she was sure Hayden could hear it.

A sense of the surreal settled over her. It was as if she'd stepped out of reality and into the pages of one of her romance novels. She decided to approach this bizarre turn of events in just that way—as if she were a character in a novel—the sexy heroine waiting to be swept off her feet by the charming hero. Or no—a brave, adventurous explorer, stepping confidently into a world she'd only glimpsed from afar.

She felt at once energized and terrified, like when she was balanced at the top of a very high, very twisty roller coaster in that split second before the plunge. She'd stepped way, way out of her comfort zone.

Was this party really worth it? Because, no question,

he was right. What they were about to do would either bring them much, much closer, or it would ruin everything. If things didn't go right, how could she still be friends with him without dying of embarrassment? How could he still be friends with her, having revealed so much of himself?

On the other hand, she'd gotten him to budge on the invitation from *absolutely not* to *maybe*. This was the chance of a lifetime, and she didn't want to spend the rest of hers regretting that she'd lost her nerve.

If only her damn hands would stop trembling. She clenched them into fists against her thighs as she waited for whatever came next. She wished she hadn't had the bright idea of getting on her knees, like one of the heroines in her novels. They never talked about how uncomfortable it was. Her bootheels were beginning to dig into her butt and her right thigh seemed to be cramping. She very much wanted to get to her feet, but she was determined to wait for Hayden's cue.

Even this moment of silence might be a test. Fine. She'd always been good at tests. She would pass this one with flying colors, and then she'd get the golden ticket—an invitation to this mysterious, exclusive club where things happened that she could barely get her head around. She couldn't decide which was more exciting—whatever was about to take place, or what it might lead to.

She focused on Hayden as she tried to still her racing thoughts. His eyes had darkened from sapphire to an even deeper blue, the lids hooding in a sexy way as his usual half-smile fell away. She expected him to rise from the sofa and extend a hand to pull her up.

Instead, he remained seated, though he leaned forward, his eyes fixed on her. "Stand up," he directed.

Dahlia got awkwardly to her feet, relieved to be off her knees. She faced him, heart pounding, mouth dry, sweat prickling in her armpits.

"Hands at your sides," he directed.

Dahlia realized she'd been twisting her fingers together, a nervous habit she thought she'd outgrown. She dropped her hands, trying to calm her jittery nerves.

"It's natural to be nervous," he said, his tone gentler now. "Close your eyes." He waited until she had obeyed.

"Focusing on your breathing will help you to calm down. I want you to take in a deep breath through your nose and let it out slowly."

Again, he waited until she had complied. "Good. Now, do that again, but this time count slowly to three as you inhale, hold it for another three seconds and then exhale to the count of three. Keep your eyes closed and keep breathing that way until I tell you to stop."

Dahlia did as he directed, feeling mildly ridiculous

standing in front of this man doing breathing exercises with her eyes closed. Yet it did help her racing heart to slow. Her shoulders, which she hadn't realized she'd been hunching, relaxed a little.

Feeling calmer, she opened her eyes and smiled. "Thanks. That did help."

He frowned. "I didn't tell you to stop, Dahlia. Or to speak. You will continue until I say so."

She very nearly protested that she was fine. They could move on. But she caught herself in time, remembering the rule about obeying him to the letter. She closed her eyes again and refocused on the breathing exercise.

In, one, two, three… Hold, one, two, three… Out, one, two, three…

Finally, he said, "Open your eyes and look at me."

She did so, both eager and nervous for whatever came next.

"From this moment until the session is over," Hayden said, his voice deepening, "you will not speak unless I ask you a direct question. The only caveat is if you want to end the session. Understood?"

Her first impulse was to protest. How did one learn without asking questions? But she reminded herself she'd agreed to this, and she was determined to see it through.

"Okay. I got it. No speaking unless spoken to."

"Good. Next directive: for the duration of the session, you will address me in a respectful tone, answering only what I ask, without embellishment or commentary. And you will address me as Sir when you respond. Do you understand?"

Dahlia was thrilled and scandalized in equal measure by this command. How did she reconcile this new version of Hayden with the progressive, sensitive man she knew? Did he really expect her to address him as if he were her boss—as if he *owned* her?

Just do it, she counseled herself. *Stop second-guessing him and just obey.*

"Yes...Sir," she managed, unable to stop the heat from rising yet again into her cheeks.

He nodded. "Good girl. I sensed your struggle just now. While I know it's tempting, don't overthink things. Don't anticipate or dissect. Just do exactly as I say, how and when I say to do it. Nothing more. Nothing less."

She had a sudden, crazy impulse to salute him and shout, "Sir-yes-sir!" like an army recruit. She'd often resorted to sarcasm when she was uncomfortable. This time, she needed to keep her mouth shut.

"Now, please remove your boots and socks if you're

wearing any, and your pants. Place the boots and socks under that chair"—he waved toward one of the chairs—"and place your pants on the seat."

It suddenly crossed her mind that this whole thing might just be an elaborate setup to get her naked. But, no, she would have happily gotten naked and fallen right into bed with this guy, despite her own personal rule of no sex on the first date. And she had a feeling he knew it.

Whatever his motives, she'd committed to this, and she was determined to see it through. If this was the price of admission, bring it on.

Striving for a calmness she didn't feel, Dahlia bent down, unzipped her ankle boots and stepped out of them. She pulled off her socks, tucking them neatly into her boots. Feeling extremely self-conscious as Hayden watched her with those sexy, hooded eyes, she undid her pants and slid them down her thighs. She was glad for the momentary reprieve as she folded and draped them over the back of the chair.

"Now, resume your position in front of me," Hayden directed, the reprieve over. "Stand with your feet shoulder-width apart and place your hands on your head."

Phew. At least he hadn't made her get all the way naked—yet.

As she assumed the position, she couldn't help but

wonder what he was going to do next.

It's just a test, she reminded herself. *To see how well you can follow orders. It's not like he's asking you to bend over and spread 'em.*

Oh, *god*. What if he *did* ask her to do that?

Don't anticipate. Just obey. She tried not to fidget. *Deep breath in...let it out...*

"Now, without moving from that position, and without stopping to think about it, tell me your most private sexual fantasy. The one you've never told anyone, not your lover, not anybody. That thing that pushes you over the edge when you're masturbating. Don't think about it too much. Just start talking."

Okay. Wait just a second here. Baring her body was one thing. She was reasonably comfortable with herself and had never been particularly shy. But did he really expect her to reveal her darkest secrets just like that?

She very nearly blurted, "Only if you go first, dude," but caught herself in time.

You can do this, she reminded herself. *"Don't forget, Hayden's made it clear he knows what he's doing when it comes to BDSM. If you want to go to the party, this is what it takes.*

And she *really* wanted to go to that party, now more than ever. She would gain entrance to a dark, secret world she'd thought only lived in the pages of novels. And anyway, surely her little sexual fantasies would be nothing to a guy like Hayden. He probably hadn't only heard it all—he'd probably done it all, as well.

She closed her eyes, trying to forget for the moment that Hayden was even in the room. She took a deep breath and then plunged in. "I wake up in the middle of the night and realize my wrists and ankles have been tied to the bedposts. I open my mouth to scream and a large, hard hand clamps over my mouth. My eyes fly open. A strange man is looming over me."

The scenario unspooled in her mind's eye, her panties moistening in a Pavlovian response to the well-worn but still effective fantasy. The handsome mystery man exuded a dark, edgy sexuality that both thrilled and frightened her. The terrifying glint of his knife in the moonlight, his warning not to move or she'd regret it, the feel of his hand on her throat, the bonds tight at her wrists and ankles, his hard, thick cock entering her...

"Go on," Hayden prompted.

"He tells me not to move. Not to scream. Then he, uh..."

Man, this was harder than she'd expected. Maybe she'd said enough? "He has his way with me," she concluded in a rush of words.

Hayden's bark of a laugh startled her. Dahlia

dropped her hands from her head, her eyes flying open in indignation.

"What?" she demanded, ignoring for the moment the requirement to only speak when spoken to. "Why are you laughing at me?"

"Come on, Dahlia," he said, his eyes dancing. "'Had his way with me?' Who under the age of seventy actually talks that way?" He shook his head. "Seriously. You started out with honesty, telling me about a very compelling fantasy that clearly has meaning for you. But then something happened, and you closed yourself off. So, let's try this again. This time, I want the truth. Unvarnished, uncensored, raw and real. From your gut, not your brain."

"But..." She trailed off, unable to refute his accusation. Heat licked not only over her face, but everywhere. Her entire body, it seemed, was blushing.

His expression gentling, Hayden got to his feet and approached her. He reached for her arms, lifting them to place her hands back on her head. The position and his proximity made her feel both terribly vulnerable and deeply aroused. Was it possible to feel both things at once?

Then he took her face gently between his hands as he stared down into her eyes. She stared back, her nipples throbbing, her sex aching. Her lips parted of their own accord, her entire being yearning for his kiss.

But instead of pressing those beautiful lips to hers, he said softly, "Don't forget who you're talking to, Dahlia. I've shared more with you about my lifestyle away from work than I ever have with someone not in the scene. I've trusted you with that. Can you trust me back, just a little? Can you accept that I make no judgments, and that I mean it when I say there is no right and wrong here? Feelings aren't actions, and fantasies are just that— fantasies."

He let her go, taking a step back. Involuntarily, she leaned forward, her skin still tingling from his touch, her unkissed lips feeling the lack.

He returned to the couch and resumed his seat. "I get it," he said. "You're not used to being so vulnerable with someone. If this is too hard, we can end—"

"No," she blurted, determined not to let him call this off, resolved not to blow it. "I can do this. I want to do this. Please...Sir."

"All right. Good. We'll continue. Close your eyes again, and this time, just let it flow."

She nodded, glad at least for the bit of distance closing her eyes provided. She recentered herself, once more stepping into the arms of her fantasy, settling back into its familiar embrace. "He has a knife. I see its silver glint in the moonlight and I feel its sharp point just below my chin. He tells me not to make a sound or he'll cut me. I believe him. My mouth is dry, my heart racing, but I'm also excited. He looks"—she stopped abruptly.

She'd been about to say, "He looks like you," but instead amended, "He's gorgeous. I can feel his power. I know I can't resist him—that I have absolutely no choice. I nod my understanding, and he sets down the knife. He cups my bare breasts and rolls my nipples between his fingers.

"'Your nipples are hard, you dirty little slut,' he says to me. He puts his hand roughly between my legs and pushes a finger inside me. I'm soaking wet."

Even as her cunt muscles spasmed at her own words, heat flamed in her face again. How was Hayden reacting to this? She wanted to open her eyes—to see his expression—but she didn't dare.

"Go on," Hayden encouraged softly. His tone was gentle, but she felt the command beneath the words, and the desire. He not only wasn't freaked out by what she was saying. He was turned on by it!

Feeling empowered by this knowledge, Dahlia found the courage to continue. "I tug at the restraints, but I can't move, not even a little. He climbs over me, and I desperately try to close my legs, but all I succeed in doing is tightening the bonds. I squeeze my eyes closed, trying to ready my body for what I know is coming. But, instead of pushing his way into me, he straddles my chest."

Dahlia swallowed and forced herself to continue, uncensored. "He shoves his big, hard cock down my throat, choking me with it. Tears are flowing down my cheeks as he pushes in and out of my mouth. Finally he pulls back and drapes his body over mine. I can't move. I don't dare protest."

She was in the zone now, barely aware Hayden was even there. "'You're nothing more than a cunt right now,' he tells me. 'A cunt that needs to be fucked. Hard.' The knife is sharp—one sudden move and he could cut my throat. He touches the point of the blade to my carotid artery and I freeze, too terrified even to breathe.

"Then he enters me in a single thrust, his laugh cruel. 'Sopping wet, you dirty little whore,' he tells me. 'You want this. You want me to do this. You're begging for it.' The crazy thing is, he's right. I do want it. In spite of what he's done to me, and his insulting words, I do want him, even though I know he's evil to the core. He swivels inside me, as hard and thick as a bar of solid steel. I can't help it. I moan…"

Dahlia trailed off, not from shyness now, but because she was caught in the fantasy, its web holding her close in its gossamer grip. If she were to touch herself now, she'd come on the spot.

"Take your hands from your head and open your eyes," Hayden commanded, bringing her back to the moment.

She opened her eyes, at first fixing them on his face. Then, unable to help herself, she let her gaze move lower down his body to his crotch. His erection was visible, bulging against the faded denim. She brought her gaze quickly back to his face.

He offered a small, knowing smile that made her look away. "Take off your sweater," he commanded, the smile still in his voice. "You can just drop it to the floor."

Dahlia obeyed, shaking out her hair after pulling the sweater over her head. She dropped it to the ground and faced him once more. Her nipples were straining against the lacey cups of her bra, the crotch of her panties sopping wet.

He raked her body once more with a slow, burning gaze, power radiating from him in an almost visible aura. "Now the bra," he said, his voice slightly hoarse.

With trembling fingers, Dahlia released the clasps at her back and let the bra fall free.

"Now the panties."

Heart high in her throat, Dahlia pulled down her panties and stepped out of them, kicking them away with her foot. Heat had returned to her face, but she stood her ground, meeting Hayden's gaze as he devoured her with his eyes.

"Hands back on your head," he said, getting to his

feet. As he approached her, her heart quickened, her breath edging into a pant.

He moved closer until he was standing directly in front of her. Then he reached for her throat, curling his fingers around her neck and squeezing ever so slightly. Dahlia's legs turned to jelly, a sudden, uncontrollable shudder moving through her frame.

Hayden stared down at her, his eyes burning into her soul.

She stared back, at once mesmerized by him, and horrified with herself. She was only supposed to get turned on by the *fantasy* of a guy tightening his grip around her throat! Fantasies, as Hayden had noted, did *not* equal reality.

What was happening? Why was she more turned on than she'd ever been in her life?

He squeezed harder, this time pulling a squawk of pure fear from Dahlia's mouth. At the same time, a dark, wild joy she didn't understand was pulsing its way through her psyche. She was trembling from head to toe. If he let her go now, she might crumple to the floor.

"You please me," he said in a low growl, his hand still tight around her throat.

In spite of her fear and confusion, a jolt of dark, raw pleasure hurtled through her bloodstream like a hit of cocaine. In spite of herself, she moaned.

All at once, he released her, at the same time bringing an arm supportively around her waist. He reached around to the back of her head, which he gently cradled in his large hand.

Every fiber of her being strained toward him as they stared at one another, his hungry expression no doubt mirroring her own.

Kiss me, she very nearly begged.

Heeding her silent plea, he dipped his head until his lips brushed hers. She sighed, her body loosening, her tongue sliding to meet his as he held her close.

Time stopped, the earth halting in its orbit as Hayden probed, teased and caressed her mouth. His hand moved in her hair, coiling it between his fingers and holding her in place in his tight grip. She lost herself in their long, perfect kiss, never wanting him to let her go.

When the pair finally parted, they were both breathless. Hayden's eyes were bright, his face lit as if from a fire within. He brushed a strand of hair from her cheek, his touch leaving a line of delicious heat on her skin.

"Congratulations, Dahlia," he said, smiling broadly. "You did very well. I definitely see an invitation in your future."

Chapter 4

Hayden's cock was hard as a rock, his mind whirling with the thrilling certainty that Dahlia was indeed a sub, if an untried one. He ached to lift her into his arms, his clothes magically dissolving as she wrapped her legs around his waist. Pushing her against a wall, he'd fuck her until she begged for mercy, until he couldn't hold on another second...

She was willing—he was sure of it. He had seen it in her eyes—that intoxicating combination of erotic fear and unbridled lust that unlocked the sensual sadist in him. He had felt it in the tremble of her limbs, in the way she'd melted against him as they'd embraced, in the hard poke of her erect nipples against his chest and the sweet, breathy sighs as they kissed...

Though it took every ounce of his self-control, Hayden forced himself to pull back. This wasn't the right time—not yet. It wouldn't be right to take her now—not when she wasn't yet his to claim.

He took another step back, harnessing his lust as he

reminded himself of his responsibilities as an ethical Dom. Placing his arm lightly around her bare shoulders, he guided her toward the couch, indicating she should sit.

"You can get dressed now," he said, retrieving and handing her clothing to her. He was pleased his voice sounded steadier than he felt. He fell onto the couch beside her.

She looked confused. "But…" she trailed off, her brow furrowing. "I don't understand. I thought we'd… After that kiss… Don't you want more? Because I do." As she said these last words, color stained her cheeks. Looking away, she clutched the bundle of clothing to her chest.

Hayden reached out, placing his hand on her warm, bare thigh. Her skin was like silk. He had to resist the urge to slide his hand higher, to cup her cunt and to press his fingers into its yielding wetness.

Keeping his hand where it was, he said gently, "I do, too, Dahlia. Believe me, I do." He glanced down at his still raging erection and flashed a grin, adding, "As you can see for yourself."

She offered a tentative smile in return, but still looked confused. Her honey hair was sexily tousled around her shoulders, her color high. The look of yearning and pure lust that lingered in her eyes very nearly broke his resolve.

He pulled his hand from her thigh before he lost control. "It wouldn't be right." His voice came out hoarse. He cleared his throat. "You've just been through a very intense experience. The parameters of that session were strictly between Dom and potential sub. If I were to make love to you now, I would be taking advantage, even if it doesn't feel that way."

He shifted so he was facing her. "Don't get me wrong—the man in me would love nothing better than to take you here and now. Your submissive grace during your very first exposure to D/s is breathtaking. It makes me want you all the more. But the Dom in me would be irresponsible to claim you when you're still caught in the throes of the experience."

He tried to think how to explain it better to someone not familiar with the scene. "It's almost like getting a girl drunk on purpose so she's more pliable. Even if she thinks she wants it, too, it's just not"—he groped for the word—"gentlemanly."

The hurt in her eyes was like a knife, poking holes in his resolve. Was he crazy not to take what this lovely girl was offering?

The tiny devil on his shoulder whispered, *Who cares if she's sub or vanilla? So what if she isn't ready yet? She's a beautiful, naked, willing woman. She wants it. You want it. Take what you've earned.*

Hayden continued to teeter precariously on that

razor's edge of a Dom's responsibility versus pure, raw desire. One push from her and he'd tumble down. God, how he longed to show her, then and there, the power and passion of a true D/s experience. Even just to take her in his arms once more—to run his fingers down her slender neck, to cup her sweet breasts, to roll her rosy nipples until they stiffened between his fingers and then to twist...

Stop it, Pierce. Get a fucking grip.

He drew in a deep breath as he again wrestled himself back under control. Lifting a metaphorical hand, he brushed the devil away.

To his relief, the pained confusion had left Dahlia's eyes. She flopped back against the sofa cushions, grabbing a pillow as she did so and hugging it to her body. "I get it," she said slowly. "It's sort of the flipside to my own policy, which is never to have sex with a guy on a first date, no matter how intense the connection feels. I've learned from experience that once that new-person-excitement vibe has worn off, as often as not you end up wondering who the hell it is in your bed, and why you ever thought you wanted him there."

"Ouch," Hayden said with a pained grin.

"Oh, not you," she said hurriedly. "I'm just saying I get it. Once I come down from this crazy high, I might end up regretting it if we move too fast."

"Exactly," Hayden agreed, relieved she understood. If she'd pressed any more, even the tiniest bit, he wasn't sure he could have resisted.

He got to his feet. "It's late, and the end of a long week. I'm actually on call tomorrow, so no telling what my schedule will be. Meanwhile, I should let you get some rest and take a little time to process the experience. Before I go, can I get you another glass of wine? A cup of tea?"

Dahlia frowned, her lower lip actually protruding slightly in an adorable pout. "Are you *sure* you can't stay?"

"I'm sure," he said emphatically.

"Okay, okay. You're probably right, anyway. This is definitely the more sensible choice." She slipped her sweater over her head, its drape over her breasts nearly undoing him once more. She, too, rose from the couch and then yawned suddenly, as if it had caught her before she could stop it.

"Oh, wow," she said with a small, tinkling laugh. "I guess I'm more wiped out than I realized." She flashed a dazzling smile. "Thanks for a truly eye-opening experience. I can honestly say this is the most *unique* first date I've ever had."

Hayden laughed. "I have to agree. But seriously, thank you for trusting not only me with this, but yourself.

I admire your courage."

She grinned. "I do feel pretty kick-butt awesome at the moment." She crossed her arms over her chest. "Now, get out of here before I change my mind and throw *you* down, cave*woman* style."

Hayden chuckled. "That'll never happen, little girl," he growled playfully. "If anyone does any throwing down, it'll be me."

"Only if I let you," she retorted.

"Precisely," he agreed. "Consent is the name of the game in D/s. Always."

He allowed her to lead him to the door. Resisting the urge to take her into his arms once more, he instead planted a kiss on the top of her head, said good night, and stepped out into the corridor.

As the door closed softly behind him, he allowed himself a sigh, part regret that he hadn't let things go further, part relief that he'd managed not to.

~*~

After Hayden left, Dahlia sank back to the couch, legs sprawled, head back against the cushions. That was, without exception, the weirdest, and the most exciting, erotic experience of her life. She still couldn't quite believe she'd gone through with it. Nor was she entirely sure how she felt about it. What was wrong with her, that she had gotten off on standing naked with her hands on her head like some kind of suspect, while a guy sat there listening to her share a sexual fantasy she'd never admitted to another soul?

She felt daring and scandalized in equal measure.

While she was delighted she had passed the test, what did her reactions to the intense session say about her as a woman? How could she possibly reconcile what she'd experienced with her sense of self?

It was too much to think about. She was exhausted, both physically and emotionally, but still jittery with excitement and pent-up lust. Why had she let Hayden go? She should have taken back the reins, ordering him to strip and service her, or get a good, hard spanking.

Just the thought made her laugh aloud. She could not imagine Hayden submitting to her or anyone. It just wasn't in his DNA. Nor did she want that from him.

What did she want?

She snorted, annoyed with herself. Could she turn off her damn analytical brain for once in her life?

She rose from the couch. Another glass of wine and a nice hot bath should help her unwind. Grabbing the rest of her clothes, she headed to the bedroom. After dropping her things, along with the sweater, onto the bed, she went into the tiny bathroom.

Leaning over the freestanding claw-foot tub, she fitted the plug, turned on the hot water and poured lavender bath oil into the water. Returning to the living room, she snagged her wineglass, draining it as she headed to the kitchen.

She poured herself more wine and carried it back with her to the bathroom. Setting the glass carefully on the ancient linoleum floor beside the tub, she climbed in and eased into the hot, fragrant water.

Reaching for the wine, she lifted the glass to her lips, taking a long sip. Leaning back with a sigh, she slid her hand into the oily water and slipped it between her legs. Closing her eyes, she imagined Hayden cradling her from behind in the tub, his hands roaming over her body. *"You belong to me,"* he growled, his hand closing around her throat.

A deep, pleasurable shudder moved through her and she let out a soft moan. Sinking deeper in the water, she imagined her fingers were his. They were on the bed now, she splayed naked in front of him. He loomed over her, his cock fisted in his hand. His eyes flashed with power and lust. "You're mine, Dahlia. I own you. Offer yourself to me. Spread your legs and beg me for it."

Fingers flying, Dahlia cried out, coming faster and harder than she ever had in her life.

"Wow," she exclaimed when she could catch her breath. "I wonder what'll happen on the *second* date."

Somehow, she got through Saturday, glad for the distraction of the usual frantic errand-running, bill paying, grocery shopping and housecleaning she reserved for the weekend. She was glad Hayden had warned her he would be at the hospital all day, so she didn't obsessively check her phone for a text or missed call.

She considered calling her best girlfriend, Naomi, to parse every moment of the date, as she normally would have done with a new guy. But each time she picked up her phone, she put it down again. While her friend was aware of Dahlia's love for BDSM romance novels, Dahlia wasn't sure she could explain what had happened the night before in terms Naomi could understand.

Shit. She could barely understand it herself. Her internal jury had deliberated overnight, and several members were now questioning her sanity.

Had she, Dahlia Simon, MD, accomplished surgeon, feminist and fiercely independent woman, actually let a guy direct her to refer to him as "Sir" and strip naked for him while he remained fully clothed, just watching?

Where was her dignity, her pride, her boundaries? It was as if he'd woven some kind of dark spell around her, getting her to do things that made her blush, even now.

No matter what he claimed, he had to be judging her now. Did he feel smug and powerful that he'd gotten her to reveal so much of herself while sharing very little in return? Had he been quietly making a fool of her? Would he laugh about it later with his Dom buddies at his secret club?

No. It hadn't been like that. And Hayden wasn't like that. He'd been as affected as she had by the bizarre "session," as he'd called it. So why the radio silence today? Yeah, she knew how insanely busy you could get on call for the hospital, sometimes not even getting a chance to pee or finish a cup of shitty coffee until hours later. But still... couldn't he have found ten seconds to shoot her a quick text?

She considered sending one to him. After all, she was just as capable as he of picking up her phone. But she decided against it. He'd been the one to leave her so abruptly. Let him be the one to contact her first.

At 10:45 that night, her phone finally pinged.

Hey there. Hope you're doing well. You were AWESOME last night. Sorry took so long to get in touch. Been at the hospital since 7:15 this morning. Non-stop crazy. Look out for a special delivery tomorrow. XXXOOO.

Not exactly a gushing declaration of love, but she wouldn't have wanted that anyway. Guys who moved too fast in the romance department had always made her nervous. She reread the text, paying more attention to the words. She thumbed back a reply.

You were pretty great yourself. Now, don't be a TEASE! What delivery?

It was twenty more minutes before he managed to reply.

Good things come to those who wait. ☺

She considered following up with more banter, but decided instead to leave it at that.

She read the message one more time, this time savoring the thrill of victory. Whatever else happened or didn't happen, she was going to the party! She jumped to her feet, as excited as a little kid just told she was going to Disneyland. "Oh, my god, oh, my god, oh, my god," she chanted as she pranced around the room. "I'm going to the party. I'm going to the party."

Sunday morning at ten o'clock Dahlia's intercom buzzed. Hurrying to it, she pressed the button. "Yes?"

"Hi, it's Matt with Eagle Courier. I have a package for you."

Dahlia, who had been lounging in her robe at the kitchen table catching up on the news, replied, "I'll be right down." She threw on a shirt and jeans, grabbed her keys and hurtled down the stairs—too excited to wait for the painfully slow elevator.

A young man in a brown uniform, AirPods in his ears, looked up as she came out of the stairwell. He held a clipboard in one hand and a large white cardboard envelope in the other. "Dr. Simon?"

"Yes. You have something for me?"

He held out the clipboard, a pen attached. "Sign here."

Dahlia scrawled her signature and he handed her the envelope.

"Have a nice day," he said without much conviction, simultaneously tapping his ear bud.

"You too," she replied, though he probably hadn't heard her.

Once back in her apartment, she raced to the couch, the envelope in hand. With trembling fingers, she tore open the tag and slid out the single page. It was printed on fine, heavy stock paper, the shiny letters raised.

We are delighted to extend you an invitation to our annual winter holiday party as a guest of Master Hayden. Due to our privacy policies, to learn more about the invitation you will first need to review and sign the legally-binding non-disclosure agreement located at our secure online site. You will find the link, as well as your one-time access code and temporary password, below.

"Master Hayden," she exclaimed aloud, both thrilled and shocked at the words. An image of Hayden decked out in full leathers, a long, evil-looking whip dangling from his hand, instantly filled Dahlia's mind.

Holy shit. Had she bitten off way the fuck more than she could chew?

"You wanted this, Dahlia," she reminded herself.

And she still did, however crazy she might be. It was an adventure of a lifetime, and no way was she going to back out now.

She hurried to the kitchen, both the invitation and its envelope in hand. Pulling her laptop closer, she typed the link in the browser, her breath shallow with excitement.

She scanned the non-disclosure agreement that filled the screen. Reading between the legalese lines, she understood the agreement bound the signatory to complete silence regarding the club's activities and existence, except with members of the club.

There followed a request to grant the club authorization to conduct a criminal background check. Dahlia raised her brows at this. She understood the need for privacy, but surely this was taking things a bit too far?

On reflection, though, it made a kind of sense. Some of the people drawn to the BDSM scene might be bullies in disguise with a history of violent acts and police involvement. Perhaps the requirement was a way to weed them out before the fact. She shrugged. Whatever the reason, she was clean as a whistle and saw no downside to granting permission. She clicked the box.

Finally, there was a place at the bottom for an electronic signature. She quickly typed in her name.

A moment later, a new screen popped up:

Thank you for executing the non-disclosure

agreement. Whether or not you choose to attend our holiday party, the terms of the agreement will remain in effect.

The Masters Club is a private, members-only BDSM venue with locations around the world. Everyone associated with the enterprise is experienced in impact play, bondage and discipline. Our membership is comprised of Doms, pleasure submissives, service submissives and 24/7 staff slaves. The holiday party will involve nudity and intense BDSM activities.

You will be escorted to our location by your host. The play party will be held in our main dungeon, with refreshments available in the auction room. While you are not required to actively participate in the events taking place, you are welcome to do so.

"Dungeon," she murmured aloud, hardly able to believe such a thing actually existed in real life. She instantly visualized naked women tethered to whipping posts and bound to spanking benches, just like in the novels. The fantasy Hayden appeared beside them, a coil of rope in one hand, a whip in the other, a dangerous glint in his dark blue eyes.

Heart beating high in her throat, she continued to read.

> Due to privacy concerns regarding our members, all attendees will be required to wear masks for the duration of the evening. We have enclosed a mask for your convenience.

She grabbed the cardboard envelope, this time popping it open and peering into it. Sure enough, something was inside. She shook the envelope and the item fell to the table. It was a shiny red masquerade mask with satin straps on either side. Picking it up, she placed it over her eyes, adjusting the nose guard as she did so.

Jumping again to her feet, she rushed to the bathroom and peered at herself in the mirror. She looked exotic and mysterious, like someone attending a masquerade ball. She had a sexy red satin cocktail dress that would go perfectly.

Removing the mask, she returned to the kitchen, settling herself once more in front of the laptop. She focused on the single, final line.

Please RSVP below.

Actually trembling with excitement, Dahlia clicked ACCEPT.

Chapter 5

Over breakfast at the hospital on Monday, Dahlia peppered Hayden with questions about the Masters Club party. He answered them all with an indulgent smile, but warned her, "It's really hard to describe to someone so new to the scene. I don't want to prejudice you in advance either way. It's better if you form your own impressions."

She wanted to press, but recognized he was probably right. Better to wait and see. After all, she was only going there to watch, not to participate. No, most definitely not.

Their usual insane work schedules prevented them from getting together during the week, which was just as well. The next time they saw each other, she wanted to experience *Master* Hayden.

The night of the party finally arrived. Dahlia pulled her shawl tighter around her shoulders, shivering as she scanned the street for Hayden's red Audi.

The sky was a dark, gunmetal gray, the reflected city lights bouncing against the heavy clouds. A light snow had begun to fall, coating everything in fairy dust.

Dahlia's heart skipped several beats as the car came into view at the end of the block. Hayden pulled to a stop in front of her building and leaned across the seat to open the passenger door.

Dahlia hurried forward from her spot beneath the building's awning, her gold high heels clicking on the sidewalk. "Ah," she said with relief as she settled herself in the passenger seat. "Nice and toasty in here."

She glanced at Hayden, who hadn't yet started driving. He was staring at her, his mouth actually hanging open. "You look...*amazing*." The awe in his tone and the look in his eye made her blush, though she couldn't deny she was pleased.

"Thank you," she said. "You clean up pretty nice yourself."

Hayden laughed as he put the car in gear. "Thanks back. I think."

Dahlia had expected him to be decked out in leather from head to toe, as befitted her concept of a Master. Instead, he was wearing a black tuxedo jacket with narrow satin lapels over a black silk T-shirt. He did have on leather pants that looked soft as butter, and seemed tailor-made to his long, muscular legs. A day or two of sexy stubble graced his strong jaw. His deep blue eyes sparkled beneath the streetlights.

He glanced at her. "Did you remember your mask?"

"Yes," she replied, patting her small clutch. "I have it right here."

"Excellent." He eased the car away from the curb.

As they headed down the block, he said, "A word about sex."

"Just one?" she quipped.

He chuckled. "Sex at the party, I mean. Because we have non-members attending tonight, explicit sexual acts—by which I mean anything that involves or potentially involves an exchange of body fluids—is not permitted. To be more direct, if somewhat crude," he added, stealing a glance at her, "there's no fucking or sucking allowed."

Dahlia immediately visualized Hayden in the middle of some Romanesque orgy, simpering slave girls kneeling around him, reaching for him with grasping hands...

"I take it that means there normally is"—she absolutely refused to blush—"fucking and sucking at regular dungeon events?"

Hayden shrugged. "Every member is routinely tested for a clean bill of health, so it's not an issue in that regard. That said, full-on intercourse is discouraged in the main dungeon. There are private playrooms for that. But oral sex is fairly common. It's often just a natural progression of a scene. You have a sub bound on a spanking bench or a bondage table, legs spread wide"—he cocked a single brow, his lips quirking into a smile—"it can be hard to resist. Conversely, if she's on her knees in front of you, arms bound behind her back, lips parted as she stares up at you, ready and eager to serve your every need..." He shrugged again, leaving the sentence incomplete.

"Good to know," Dahlia managed with what she hoped was a nonchalant tone.

They were silent after that, Hayden fully focused on the road. She watched him as he drove, admiring his strong profile. He seemed so casual about all this, like it was an everyday thing and no big deal. But that actually was the case, wasn't it? He'd made it clear—he was a member of a club where literally dozens of available women who shared his kink waited at his beck and call. Was a guy like this, one who apparently moved so freely from one woman to the next, really someone she wanted to get involved with? Was she out of her mind to have let things even get this far?

Okay, stop it right now, she ordered herself. *Who ever said a word about getting involved? You're having an adventure, that's all. Whatever might or might not happen going forward is neither here nor there.*

The snow was falling more heavily now, some of it sticking to the asphalt. Dahlia lost track of where they were as Hayden weaved expertly amidst the traffic. She got her bearings again when they entered Greenwich Village, the high marble arch that opened onto Washington Square Park now visible in the near distance.

They entered a narrow, cobblestoned lane, bare-limbed trees along one side, a high stone wall on the other. The lane was softly lit by old-fashioned streetlamps, snowflakes dancing in their glow. Both sides of the short block were lined with parked cars.

"Here we are," Hayden said. "The Masters Club, my home away from home."

Dahlia glanced out the window, confused. "Where?"

He grinned. "Behind that wall there. Just another layer of privacy between us and the vanilla world." He turned into a narrow alley, revealing a freestanding brownstone, the warm glow of lights beckoning from the windows. "We own the building," Hayden explained as he drove down a wide, sloping driveway. "It houses the club and some of the full-time staff." He approached a six-car garage, adding, "These used to be stables back in the day. Now it's just a garage."

"And you're one of the lucky six who has a space here?" Dahlia asked, impressed.

He shrugged. "One of the perks of being a Head Master."

"Headmaster?" Dahlia echoed, confused.

"Not like a principal," Hayden replied with a laugh. "Though the uninitiated understandably might think that. It's two separate words, and all it means is that I'm one of the primary members of the Masters Club. I help with policy decisions and membership admission, and I assist in the selection process when we're auditioning potential pleasure subs and service slaves."

"Oooh," Dahlia exclaimed, scandalized and titillated in equal measure. "Audition process! Like what you did with me?"

He glanced at her, his expression amused. "Sweetheart, what I did with you was like dipping your toe in a baby pool. To keep the metaphor going, potential service slaves and even the pleasure subs members are expected to dive from an Olympic-height board into the deep end, arms bound behind their backs. They undergo a rigorous and purposely stressful series of tests to get their full measure."

"Huh," Dahlia said, some of the wind taken out of her sails. "Sounds like all the onus is on them. Do the Doms have to go through a similar process?"

"Not precisely," Hayden replied. "Dominant members pay a steep fee to join, and ongoing maintenance fees to cover costs. Before they can join, they, too, undergo a kind of audition, though with a different focus. Each potential member is subjected to an extensive background check. Then they are fully assessed for their skill, dedication to the lifestyle and responsible behavior in the community. As I mentioned before, the Masters Club isn't just some swingers' club with S&M trappings. We're passionate about what we do, in every sense of the word."

"It's a wonder you have time for your day job," Dahlia quipped.

"I couldn't agree more," Hayden said with a laugh. "Good thing I don't need much sleep."

He turned to her with a smile. "Forget all that stuff for now. Our main agenda tonight is to have fun." He touched something on the visor and one of the garage doors slowly lifted. They drove into one of two remaining vacant spots and he cut off the engine.

"Ready?"

Dahlia's stomach twisted with nervous anticipation and excitement. "As ready as I'll ever be."

Reaching into his jacket, Hayden produced an eye mask like the one she'd received with the invitation. Instead of red, it was shiny black with a trace of gold glitter at the edges. "Time for our masks," he said, placing it over his eyes and nose.

Dahlia reached into her purse, glad now of the disguise, such as it was. Hopefully, it would hide her nerves along with her face.

Hayden was around the side of the car before she'd finished tying the satin ribbons behind her head. He opened the door and held out his hand to her. Charmed, she took it.

As before, the feel of his skin on hers sent a delicious electric tingle through her body. Whatever happened tonight, she'd have Hayden—Master Hayden—by her side.

Walking past the other cars, they entered the building, stepping into a narrow hallway. She could see a large kitchen to their left and hear the sounds of clanging pots, clinking glasses and muffled conversation from within.

"This way," Hayden said, lightly taking her elbow. "Let's have a quick drink before we go up to the dungeon."

They moved down a hallway that opened onto an imposing, marble-floored foyer. This led into a large, elegantly appointed room filled with fine, leather-upholstered furniture, the hardwood floor scattered with Persian rugs. There was a beautiful old stone fireplace, a welcoming fire crackling within. A long table stood against one wall, heaped with plates and trays of various hors d'oeuvres and pastries. The air was scented with fresh pine needles, spiced cider and cinnamon.

Dahlia caught her breath as she took in the scene. There were maybe twenty people scattered about the space, many holding champagne flutes or brandy snifters, some with small plates of food balanced in their hands. All of them wore masquerade masks in black, red or royal blue. Many were clad from head to toe in black leather. Others, mostly women, were naked or nearly so, some of them kneeling on large floor cushions. It looked like the set of some elaborate X-rated film.

She gasped in shock when she saw a young woman with a shaved head, naked save for a collar with a leash dangling between her bare breasts. There wasn't a trace of hair anywhere on her body. Her skin was crisscrossed with long welts, some fresh, some fading. She was locked into a tall cage, her fingers curled around the bars, her large eyes moving restlessly around the room.

Dahlia suddenly found it difficult to breathe. Was the girl hurt? Who had done this to her? Why did no one else seem to care?

Hayden's warm voice, along with his steadying hand still on her elbow, broke into her thoughts. "Would you like a drink? Hot cider, champagne, brandy? Perhaps something to eat?"

Ignoring his question, she said urgently, "Look over there. That woman in the cage, she's hurt! She needs medical attention. What the hell is going on here? Why does no one seem to notice or care?"

Hayden followed her gaze. To her surprise, instead of sharing her outrage, he said calmly, "It's okay, Dahlia. Calm down. That's Belinda. She belongs to Master Robert, that guy over there." He gestured toward a tall man standing near the cage in conversation with a statuesque woman with swept-up silver hair. Both wore black masks.

"I know Robert and Belinda well," Hayden continued. "They've been happily married for at least five years now. And don't worry. Those welts are badges of courage, marks of honor, given with love and accepted with grace. Her head is shaved because she requested it of her Master. She says it's a testament of her refusal to hide anything of herself from him. As to being in the cage, she adores being confined, and always asks, when they spend any time in the auction room before dungeon play, to be placed there to help her get in a better submissive headspace. In other words," he added, his eyes kind, "she's exactly where she wants to be."

Dahlia nodded slowly as she absorbed this. She was glad to be reminded the arrangement was fully consensual, but it still didn't sit right with her. She'd read about this sort of thing in books, and even in testimonials on the internet, but somehow seeing it in real life was quite another thing. Who in their right mind would choose to subjugate themselves to such a degree? When did so-called submission edge into the murky waters of outright abuse?

As if reading her mind, Hayden said, "Don't forget our core tenet, Dahlia. We practice RACK here at the club—risk-aware *consensual* kink. While it can be edgy, even extreme, limits are always strictly observed. Sometimes the sub involved wants, or thinks they want, more than the Dom deems is safe. It's up to him to set those limits, while still giving his sub the intensity of experience she craves."

He placed a comforting hand on Dahlia's lower back. "What might be extreme to you—dangerous even—is exactly what gives someone else's life meaning. BDSM is a spectrum. It can take many forms. Erotic pain can encompass everything from a light spanking to an intense caning to blood play to skin scarification."

"Jesus," Dahlia murmured. Who the hell was this guy? How did she reconcile the wisecracking, easygoing physician she'd come to know at the hospital with this dark, edgy Master who enjoyed inflicting pain, erotic or otherwise?

Lighten up, she told herself. She didn't have to make any decisions tonight. She was merely there to observe. She would just take things as they came, drinking it all in.

Turning firmly away from the caged woman, she offered Hayden a smile. "How about that drink you promised?"

He bowed in an exaggerated way that made her giggle. "Right this way, ma'am."

They moved toward a bar set up in a corner of the room. A bare-breasted woman stood behind it, ladling hot cider into a mug for an older gentleman in a red silk dinner jacket, a black mask covering the top half of his wrinkled face. Though the young woman's eyes and nose were covered by a blue mask, it was still evident she was quite a beauty.

Dahlia tried not to ogle the woman, but couldn't seem to look away. Her nipples were pierced with gold hoops and she wore a deep blue collar around her neck, small O-rings attached at intervals. Tiny red Christmas ornaments had been attached to each O-ring in a nod to the season, Dahlia supposed. The girl wore matching leather cuffs on her wrists.

"Good evening, Alex," Hayden said to the man. "It's nice to see you out tonight. Happy holidays." He nodded toward the naked bartender. "Hello, Charlotte."

"Welcome, Sir," she replied in a high, sweet voice.

"Hayden, my boy," Alex boomed heartily. "A happy new year to you. It's good to see you." He turned to Dahlia, looking her brazenly up and down. "And who is this beauty you've brought? No Masters Club's collar, I see. Is she yours?"

Dahlia was slightly taken aback by this man referring

to her in the third person when she was standing right there. On the other hand, it did give her a moment to observe Hayden in his element without having to directly participate.

A subtle shift had come over him when they'd entered the old brownstone. He seemed taller somehow, and carried himself with a more confident stride than she'd seen before. He seemed more "present," if that even made any sense. If he were an image on screen, it would have been as if he'd suddenly been clicked into focus. Clearly, the man was in his element.

"Dahlia is a friend of mine," Hayden replied easily. "A non-member."

"Ah," Alex replied, touching the side of his mask and giving her a wink. "Welcome to the Masters Club. I hope you enjoy yourself tonight."

"Thank you," Dahlia managed, pleased her voice came out reasonably steady.

As the older man drifted away, Charlotte handed them each a flute of champagne. They clinked glasses and then Hayden downed his in a single gulp. Dahlia sipped more slowly, the dry, bubbly wine going down easily.

Setting his glass on the bar, Hayden asked, "Want something to eat before we go up to the dungeon?"

Though the food looked delicious, there was no way in the world she could eat a thing. She was way too nervous and excited to even consider it.

"Thanks. Maybe later." She drained the last of her champagne. Setting down her glass, she smoothed her short dress over her thighs and blew out a breath.

"I'm ready," she said with a confidence she didn't feel. "Let's go."

Chapter 6

Hayden took Dahlia up the wide, curving staircase to the second floor. Directly across the landing stood the double doors that led into the main dungeon. He could feel her tension, and her excitement, as they stopped at the doors.

He turned to her, stroking one of the tendrils of blond hair that hung in a soft curl on her cheek. She was wearing a slinky red dress that hugged her lovely curves, the hem high enough on her thighs to reveal her long, shapely legs, the effect enhanced by the sexy high heels. The cashmere gold shawl draped around her shoulders brought out the green in her large hazel eyes. The only thing missing was a leather collar around that long, slender neck.

Her lush mouth was painted a bright, shiny red, like an apple begging to be bitten. His lips tingled with the need to kiss her. He resisted a sudden urge to take the shawl from her and use it to tie her hands behind her back.

While he couldn't deny his intense and growing attraction to Dahlia, she was still something of an unknown when it came to D/s. And, though he understood the need for anonymity when non-members were in attendance, the mask would be a hindrance to his ability to assess her reactions and emotions.

Not that he was going in blind. Based on her powerful reactions to their initial session, he was certain she had a definite submissive streak, one he'd love to explore. But what about erotic pain? Where did this intriguing woman fall on that particular scale? Would he be the one to find out?

He pulled open one of the doors. Placing his hand lightly on the small of her back, he guided her into the main dungeon. She stopped just inside, her body going rigid as she took in the scene.

"Oh my god," she breathed, the words infused with a kind of thrilled horror.

Had this been a terrible mistake? Was he exposing Dahlia to something she wasn't yet ready to see?

He shook his head. He was not a man to second-guess himself and had no intention of starting now. She'd cajoled and pleaded her way to an invitation and, to be fair, had earned the right. He'd prepared her as best he could for what she was about to see. She was going into it with eyes wide open. If she turned around right now and said she wanted to leave, that would be that.

But she didn't turn. Instead, she moved her head slowly, taking it all in. Hayden swelled with proprietary pride as he viewed the place through her eyes. As BDSM dungeons went, this one was top notch. They had everything from simple spanking benches, St. Andrew's crosses and bondage tables to a custom-made bondage wheel and a state-of-the-art water submersion tank, along with various diabolical torture racks and devices that added delightful variety and endless possibilities.

It seemed the entire New York membership had turned out for the party, along with quite a few guests. Forty or so people were already in the dungeon, with many scenes in progress at the various stations set up all around the large space. Cries of pain and moans of pleasure filled the air, which crackled with lust and power.

A row of lovely, naked pleasure subs knelt along one wall, waiting to be tapped for play. Others were bound to crosses, tethered to whipping posts or secured on benches and padded tables, their Masters before them taking their sadistic pleasure.

Dahlia was staring, her eyes wide behind the mask, a hand to her mouth. "Oh, my god," she whispered again. "Is this for real?"

"As real as it gets," Hayden confirmed, offering a reassuring smile. "Just remember, everyone here is exactly where they want to be."

She fixed her gaze on a woman suspended upside down on a restraint rack, her legs spread wide. The Dom behind her was snapping his single tail over her inner thighs. When the lash flicked over her bared cunt, she cried out.

"Jesus," Dahlia exclaimed. "She actually *likes* that?"

"Like isn't the word I'd choose. Crave would be more accurate. Require." He placed a comforting hand on Dahlia's shoulder. "Make no mistake. Sexual masochists certainly feel pain. The difference between them and their vanilla counterparts is what happens a moment after, as that pain shifts into something deeper and more intense than you can imagine. When a sub is able to truly let go, that erotic pain lifts them to a different sphere of existence. Some say they feel like they've left their body behind, rising to some ephemeral, higher plane. From what I've personally observed, it's more like they inhabit them more fully, feeling every breath, every touch, every stroke of the skin and brush of the lips with an intensity it's hard to fathom."

She turned her head from the scene to face him. Even with the mask, he could see the change in her demeanor. There was a softening in her expression, a look of genuine longing in her lovely eyes. "Wow. It sounds so intense."

Hayden clenched his hands into fists at his sides to keep from pulling her into his arms then and there. How he wanted to rip that flimsy dress from her body and lock her into a St. Andrew's cross so he could mark that virgin flesh with stinging leather. But first, he would bend her over his knee so he could spank that luscious ass until it was cherry red. Then he'd shift her so she was straddling his thighs. Kissing her tear-stained cheeks, he would ease his cock into that hot, wet cunt...

"Hayden?" Dahlia queried, jerking Hayden from his fantasy. She was regarding him with a quizzical look. "Are you okay?"

He blinked and managed a grin. He didn't bother to hide the erection now bulging at his crotch. "I'm fine. How about you? Are you ready to see what all the fuss is about? As long as there's no privacy screen in place, onlookers are welcome."

"Lead the way," she replied.

He brought her first to one of the tamer scenes in progress. Even behind their masks, the pair was easy to recognize. Julia, a striking, dark-skinned woman with large, round breasts, was bound to the cross, a bright-red ball gag thrust between her teeth. Her lovely nipples were trapped in the grip of a pair of clover clamps, the silver chain that linked them swaying below. Her husband, Oscar, moved slowly around the cross, expertly flicking a multi-tressed flogger over every inch of Julia's naked body.

Dahlia stood at the edge of the scene station, still as

a statue. She barely seemed to be breathing. Her nipples were visible beneath her dress, round little berries he wanted to bite. He could sense both tension and desire in her bearing. He wanted to press her—to demand she tell him exactly how she was feeling at that precise moment, holding nothing back.

He stopped himself. Dahlia was there as his guest, not his submissive. He was well aware how easy it could be for a Dom to sway a sub to his desires, especially an untrained, untested sub like Dahlia. He needed to give her space to come to her own conclusions.

After a while, he reached for her hand, giving it a gentle squeeze. "Ready to move on?" he murmured in her ear.

Dahlia shook her head suddenly, as if emerging from a trance. "What? Oh. Yes, okay."

He took her next to a station where a male sub was bound spread-eagle on a bondage table, two Dommes standing over him with candles. They'd been at it awhile, as much of his torso was covered in red wax. When several scalding drops landed directly on his erect cock, the guy winced and then cried, "Thank you, Mistress. Please, may I have another?" Several more drops landed on his cock and balls.

"It's so weird," Dahlia murmured, leaning close to Hayden. "That's got to hurt like hell in the second it's happening, but you can tell he's really, really into it." She shook her head. "I'm not sure I get that."

Turning to face her, Hayden ran a finger lightly along the side of her neck. Then he eased his hand over her throat, catching it lightly in his grip.

Dahlia shivered at his touch, her eyes widening behind the mask, her lips parting as she stared up at him. "Oh," she sighed, a sweet, yielding look suffusing her features.

Leaning down so his mouth was close to her ear, Hayden murmured, "For him, it's hot wax, for you"— he added just a touch of tension to his grip—"it's a strong hand around your throat, a primal gesture of dominant control that speaks to the submissive inside you."

Dahlia made a soft sound in her throat as she stared up at him. She made no move to stop him, or to pull away. He could feel her excitement and nervous energy, as if it were an actual electrical current buzzing along her skin. How he wanted to squeeze tighter, and then tighter still, not releasing her until it pleased him to do so. She would stare up at him with wild eyes, her face reddening, her heart hammering, her nipples engorged, her cunt soaking wet. He would take her to the very edge, cutting off her ability to breathe, her very life in his hands...

Hayden abruptly let her go and took a step back before he lost control. Dahlia didn't move for several seconds.

Then, as if once more emerging from a trance, she tossed her hair and gave a small laugh. "Got it. Different strokes for different folks." She turned away, facing the dungeon at large. "What's next?" she asked. He got the impression she was going for strident, even cocky, but a slight quaver in her voice belied her words.

He brought her next to one of his personal favorites, the bondage wheel. A small crowd had gathered, making it impossible for them to stand side-by-side. Instead, Hayden gestured for Dahlia to stand just in front of him, as he could easily see over her head.

He recognized Cameron Lord with his partner, Jess. She was bound to the wheel, her wrists and ankles tethered to the circumference, forcing her into a human X. Her long, coppery auburn hair hung in loose curls past her shoulders. Her body gleamed with sweat. She wore nothing but her slave collar and a red leather thong that barely covered her sex.

Brandon, one of the house slaves, was spinning her slowly in a full circle as Cameron snapped his thin, whippy cane over her fair skin, already streaked with pink welts.

"Oh, my god," Dahlia cried softly, bringing her hands to her mouth. Hayden moved closer until his chest was pressed against her back. He could feel her heart beating fast as a hummingbird's wings against his chest.

She leaned back into him as he brought his arms

around her waist. They watched together in silence as Cameron expertly snapped the whistling cane against Jess's body, while Brandon continued to turn the wheel.

When Cameron tapped the cane against Jess's inner thighs in a rapid series of stinging strokes, she cried out for the first time, her eyes bright with tears behind the mask.

Dahlia stiffened against Hayden, her breathing audible. "Oh my god," she said breathlessly, the shock evident in her tone and the sudden rigidity in her body.

"Shh," he murmured into her ear. "It's okay. He knows what he's doing."

As if he'd heard Hayden, Cameron paused. "Do you want me to stop, darling?"

"No, Sir," Jess breathed fervently. "Please, no, Sir. I'm almost there…" She trailed off in a sigh, her eyes fluttering shut.

"Yes," Cameron crooned in response. He flicked the tip of the cane over her already-marked breasts, each flick drawing a low, primal moan from Jess's lips. Then it happened—Jess's breathing slowed and deepened, every bit of lingering tension leaving her body as her head fell back.

Cameron dropped the cane and moved closer to her. He gently stroked her face as he murmured in her ear. Jess didn't move a muscle or make a sound. A kind of deep peace shimmered around her, almost palpable in the air.

At a nod from Cameron, Brandon at once crouched to release her ankles, while Cameron freed her wrists. As Jess fell forward, Cameron gathered her into his arms. Cradling her against his chest, he brought his mouth to hers. She circled her arms around his neck as they kissed. The lingering onlookers burst into spontaneous applause, and even Dahlia sighed happily.

As he watched the pair, so obviously in love, Hayden experienced a sudden spasm of pure jealousy that was new to him. As powerful as BDSM was for him, he'd never felt that kind of connection with anyone.

He'd never *wanted* that kind of connection, he reminded himself. That was a huge part of why he'd worked himself up to the rank of Head Master. He got his pick of every lovely slave girl and sub who crossed the threshold. Why limit himself to just one woman, when there were literally dozens ready and eager to submit?

Anyway, this evening wasn't about him. Far more important was Dahlia's reaction. It was evident she'd been strongly affected by everything she'd seen. He was convinced now, more than ever, that she was a natural— a submissive diamond in the rough.

"Let's take a break," he suggested, placing an arm around her shoulders.

"Yes," she agreed with a small laugh. "All I did was watch, but for some reason, I'm wiped out."

"It's a lot to process," Hayden agreed as they made their way to a quiet corner where a privacy screen had been set up. Dropping his arm from her shoulder, he reached back and untied the satin ribbons that held his mask in place.

"It's okay as long as we stay back here," he said. "You can take yours off, too."

With a nod, she untied her mask. Her cheeks were flushed, her eyes bright. Her lips glistened in the soft light, the tip of her pink tongue just visible on her lower lip. He was excited to hear in her own words how strongly the scenes had affected her. Maybe she'd even ask him, then and there, for a scene of their own.

"So," he said, keeping his tone light, "what do you think so far? Pretty powerful stuff, huh?"

"Holy cow," she blurted, charming him with the old-fashioned phrase. "It was something else, all right. I had no idea this kind of thing actually happened in real life, and on such a scale. I admit, I'm fascinated and more than a little intrigued."

"All good," Hayden replied, encouraged by her words.

But then she wrapped her arms around her torso,

some of the light leaving her eyes. Looking past him, she said, "I really appreciate your letting me get a glimpse of your world. But it's not for me." She tossed her hair, meeting his eyes, something like defiance in her face. "No," she said, a sudden quaver entering her voice again as her eyes skittered away from his. "Definitely not for me."

Hayden stared at her, taken aback by her abrupt about-face. What the hell…?

Then he grinned, getting it. He was genuinely amused at her denial in the face of such overwhelming evidence to the contrary. But no way in hell was he going to let her get away with it.

"You're lying, sexy girl." As he said the words, their truth resonated in his bones.

"Oh, yeah?" she retorted with a saucy toss of her hair. But not before he saw the sudden flash of longing in those beautiful eyes. It was as if she were silently begging him to break through her defenses once and for all.

Hayden reached for Dahlia, cupping the back of her head with one hand and circling her waist with the other. He dipped his head, bringing his mouth to hers. With a sigh, she parted her lips, and their tongues met. As he pulled her close, she melted into him, her nipples poking hard against his chest. She tasted sweet, like champagne with a hint of orange. Her skin smelled of jasmine and pure animal lust.

He found the hairpins that held her loose twist in place. As her thick, soft hair tumbled down, he gripped a handful and gave it a sharp tug, forcing her head farther back.

She gasped against his mouth in that sweet combination of pain and deep longing he knew well. But she didn't pull away. If anything, her kiss became more ardent. When he finally let her go, her chest was heaving, her eyes shining.

"Oh, Hayden," she whispered, both fear and longing on her face. "Maybe you're right, just a little bit. Maybe there's a place for me in your world. I just don't know…" She trailed off, looking away.

Gently, he reached for her, cradling her cheek in his hand as he drew her gaze back to him. "I do," he asserted. "And I'm going to prove it."

TO READ THE CONTINUING STORY OF HAYDEN AND DAHLIA, BE SURE TO GET THE FULL-LENGTH NOVEL – *MORE THAN A DARE!*

ABOUT THE AUTHOR

Claire Thompson has been writing for nearly two decades and has published over 80 novels, focusing on BDSM romance and non-con abduction tales, spanning both m/f and m/m genres. She has received numerous awards for her bestselling work, including the Golden Flogger BDSM Novel of the Year and the NLA-Int'l Pauline Réage Award for best BDSM fiction.

Claire's darker work presses the envelope of eroticism and what can sometimes be a dangerous slide into the world of sadomasochism. Ultimately, her work deals with the human condition and our constant search for love and intensity of experience.

Would you like to try an erotic romance? Or maybe you crave something dark and dangerous? Why choose when you can have it all?

Join my mailing list, pick the types of books YOU enjoy, and receive a Claire Thompson starter library based on your interests. Follow this link for more info on the starter library books.
https://mailchi.mp/clairethompson.net/mailing_list_signup